SOP   ACS   6/96

AESOP'S FABLES

PUBLISHER'S NOTE

THE Design which forms the Frontispiece to this Book, and which is therefore presumed to be somewhat typical of the intention of Fable, represents Man tried at the Court of the Lion for the ill-treatment of a Horse. It will be seen that Man has the worst of it: while his Victim has secured the Shark for his Solicitor, and the Fox, Ape, and Vulture for Counsel; the woe-begone Defendant has had to make shift with Wolf, Dog, Ass, and Daw. The Rat and the Rabbit, the Elephant and the Sheep, even the Turkey and the little Birds, seem to have given it against him, irrespective of the "Silence" of the Parrot Usher. The Clerk of the Arraigns looks through his spectacles, and the Bull has gone to sleep in a corner.

THE FABLES OF ÆSOP

AND OTHERS

TRANSLATED INTO HUMAN NATURE

DESIGNED AND DRAWN ON THE WOOD

BY

CHARLES. H. BENNETT

WITH ADDITIONAL FABLES
DESIGNED AND DRAWN
BY
RANDOLPH CALDECOTT

BRACKEN BOOKS
LONDON

This edition published 1986 by Bracken Books
a division of Bestseller Publications Ltd
Princess House, 50 Eastcastle Street, London W1N 7AP

ISBN 1 85170 067 6

Manufactured by CT Products, London, England

CONTENTS

THE WOLF AND
THE LAMB

AS a hungry thief of a Wolf was loitering at the end of a lonely road, there passed by a mild-faced timid-looking Lamb, who was returning to the maternal pen. As the Lamb wore a fine fleecy coat, and carried about him many signs of good living, the marauder's jaws watered at the prospect of a supper.

"What do you mean," said he, glaring upon the little traveller with his fierce eyes, "by taking up so much of the path where I am walking?"

The Lamb, frightened at the Wolf's angry tone and terrible aspect, told him that, with all due submission, he could not conceive how his walking on such a wide path could occasion him any inconvenience.

"What!" exclaimed the Wolf, seemingly in great anger and indignation; "you are as impudent as your father, the magistrate's dog, with the letters on his collar, who seized me by the throat last year, and caused me to be kept in a cage for three months – having all my beautiful hair cut off!"

"If you will believe me," said the innocent Lamb, "my parents are poor simple creatures who live entirely by green stuffs, in Lambeth Walk, hard by; we are none of us hunters of your species."

"Ah! I see it's no use talking to you," said the Wolf, drawing up close to him; "it runs in the blood of your family to hate us Wolves; and therefore as we have come so conveniently together, I'll just pay off a few of your forefathers' scores before we part."

So saying, he lept at the throat of the poor pet Lamb from behind, and garotted him with his own pretty gold-studded collar.

THE WOLF AND THE LAMB.

THE FROG AND THE OX

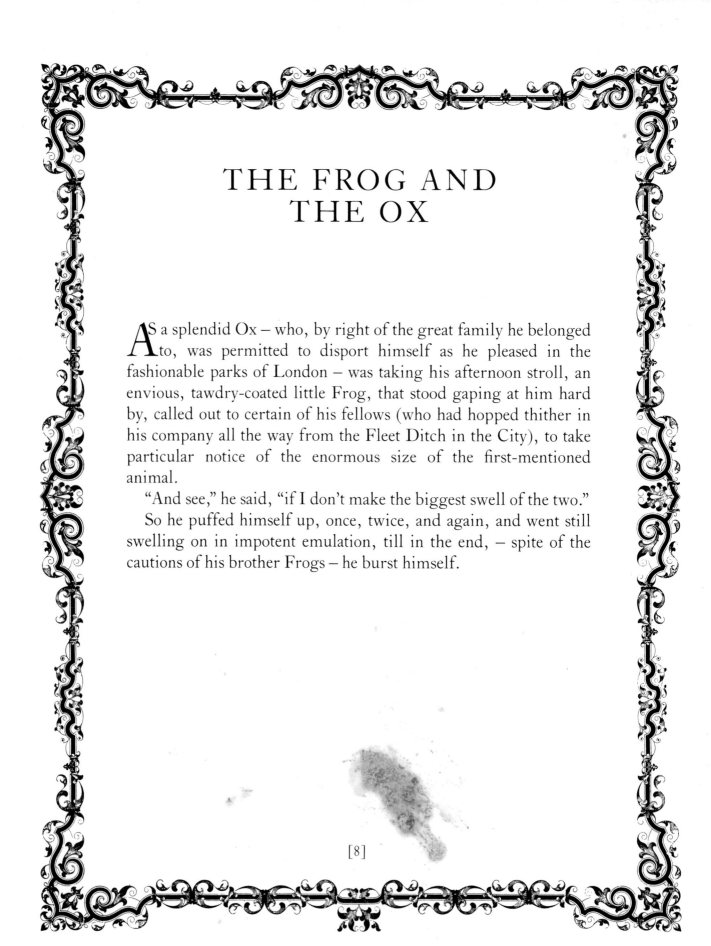

AS a splendid Ox – who, by right of the great family he belonged to, was permitted to disport himself as he pleased in the fashionable parks of London – was taking his afternoon stroll, an envious, tawdry-coated little Frog, that stood gaping at him hard by, called out to certain of his fellows (who had hopped thither in his company all the way from the Fleet Ditch in the City), to take particular notice of the enormous size of the first-mentioned animal.

"And see," he said, "if I don't make the biggest swell of the two."

So he puffed himself up, once, twice, and again, and went still swelling on in impotent emulation, till in the end, – spite of the cautions of his brother Frogs – he burst himself.

THE FROG AND THE OX.

THE ASS
IN A LION'S SKIN

THERE was a dreadful young Ass once, who prevailed upon the old Asses, his indulgent parents, to obtain for him a Lion's skin, in which to masquerade about the world. At great cost and inconvenience to themselves, they provided him with the disguise he had begged for; and, clothed in it, he strutted forth believing himself a very Lion, and causing men to flee before him in terror.

But it chanced in the end that, partly by the length of his ears, and partly by the discordance of his bray when he tried roaring, he was discovered, and the Lions with whom he had sought to herd fell upon him so mercilessly, that he only saved himself by flight, leaving his brave coat behind him, while men on every side laughed at and pelted him as he flew to his native common.

THE ASS IN A LION'S SKIN.

THE FISHERMAN AND
THE LITTLE FISH

A FISHERMAN cast his net and caught a little Fish. The little Fish begged him to let him go for the present, as he was so small, and to catch him again to more purpose later on, when he was bulkier. But the Fisherman said: "Nay, I should be a very simpleton to let go a good thing I have got and run after a doubtful expectation."

THE LOBSTER AND
HIS MOTHER

A GREENISH young Lobster crawling along the Strand with his mother (who, being old and learned, had attained to a deep blue complexion), was struck by the appearance of a specimen of his own tribe – evidently laid out for show – whose shell-jacket was of a brilliant red. Young, ignorant, and vain, he viewed the dazzling spectacle with admiration and envy.

"Behold," he said, addressing his parent, "the beauty and splendour of one of our family, thus decked out in glorious scarlet. I shall have no rest till I am possessed of an appearance equally magnificent. How can I bear to see myself the dingy object I am at present, mingling undistinguished with our race?"

"Proud and heedless idiot!" replied the hard old lady, "this same tawdry finery, you so earnestly covet, is but too easily obtained. In order to possess this appearance, *it is only necessary to be boiled*."

THE LOBSTER AND HIS MOTHER.

THE WOLVES AND
THE SICK ASS

THERE were certain hungry carrion-hunting Wolves, who, in a qualm of wonderful charity, paid a visit to a fat old Ass, who lay ill of a bean-surfeit, and was like to die.

"Pray, my good friend," said they, after many protestations of regard, "whereabouts is your greatest pain?"

"Oh, gently! gently!" replied the Ass, as they proceeded to feel his pulse, "for it pricks me just there, where you lay your fingers."

THE WOLVES AND THE SICK ASS.

THE APE AND
HER TWO YOUNG ONES

THERE was a foolish old widowed She-Ape, who had two young Monkeys of twins. She doted upon one of them, whom she countenanced in breaking and pilfering what he pleased; while she only noticed the other to punish him bitterly if he should aggrieve or thwart his brother, but on the whole left him to his own devices.

In the end the spoiled favourite broke out of bounds, and committed a theft away from his mother's cage, and was snapped at by a big Watch-Dog, whose kennel was in a neighbouring Court; while his neglected brother grew up a harmless, active, and amusing Monkey, much respected by all who knew him.

THE APE AND HER TWO YOUNG ONES.

THE STAG LOOKING INTO THE WATER

A STAG parched with thirst came to a spring of water. As he was drinking he saw his own reflection on the water, and was in raptures with his horns when he observed their splendid size and shape, but was troubled about his legs, they seemed so thin and weak. As he was still musing, some huntsmen with a pack of hounds appeared and disturbed him, whereupon the Stag took to flight, and keeping a good distance ahead so long as the plain was free from trees, he was being saved; but when he came to a woody place he got his horns entangled in the branches, and being unable to move was seized by the hounds. When he was at the point of death he said to himself: "What a fool am I, who was on the way to be saved by the very things which I thought would fail me; while by those in which I so much trusted I am brought to ruin."

THE DAW
IN BORROWED PLUMES

A RICH vulgar Daw, who had a mind to be genteel, tricked herself out in all the gay feathers which fell from the fashionable Peacocks, and upon the credit of these borrowed ornaments valued herself above all the birds of the air. But this absurd vanity got her the envy of all the high-born birds with whom she wished to associate; who, indeed, upon the discovery of the truth, by common consent fell to pluming her, and when each bird had taken her own feather, this silly Daw had nothing left wherewith to cover her naked vulgarity.

THE DAW IN BORROWED PLUMES.

THE LION AND
THE GNAT

AS a great majestic Lion was gathering himself up within his lair, to astonish mankind with the wondrous powers of his roar, there came buzzing under his very nose a troublesome Gnat, who challenged him to combat.

"What avail your tremendous lungs and cavernous throat, compared to the melodious pipes of my little organ? and as for your strength, endurance, and resolution, I defy you to put that point to an issue at once."

The Lion finding the insect would not be brushed away, was fain to accept the challenge; so to it they went. But the Lion had no chance, for the Gnat charged direct into the drum of the Lion's ear, and there twinged him until in very despair he tore himself with his own paws. In the end the Gnat gained the victory over the noble beast, upon which he flew away, but had the misfortune afterwards in his flight to strike into a cobweb, where he, the conqueror, fell a prey to a large Blue-bottle Spider.

THE LION AND THE GNAT.

THE FOX AND
THE CROW

A HOMELY old female Crow, having flown out of a shop in the town with a piece of rich cheese in her bill, betook herself to a fine eminence in the country, in order to enjoy it; which a cunning Fox observing, came and sat at her feet, and began to compliment the Crow upon the subject of her beauty.

"I protest," said he, "I never observed it before, but your feathers are of a more delicate white than any I ever saw in my life! Ah, what a fine shape and graceful turn of the body is there! And I make no question but you have a voice to correspond. If it is but as fine as your complexion, I do not know a bird that can pretend to stand in competition with you. Come, let me hear you exercise it by pronouncing a single mono-syllable, which will bind me to you, hand and heart for ever."

The Crow, tickled with this very civil language, nestled and wriggled about, and hardly knew where she was; but thinking the Fox had scarcely done justice to her voice, and wishing to set him right in that matter, she called out "Yes," as loud as possible. But, through this one fatal mistake of opening her mouth, she let fall her rich prize – (in the Fox's shrewd estimation all she was worth in the world) – which the Fox snapped up directly, and trotted away to amuse himself as he pleased, laughing to himself at the credulity of the Crow, who saw but little of him or her cheese afterwards.

THE FOX AND THE CROW.

THE LION AND
OTHER BEASTS

THE Lion one day went out hunting along with three other Beasts, and they caught a Stag. With the consent of the others the Lion divided it, and he cut it into four equal portions; but when the others were going to take hold of their shares, "Gently, my friends," said the Lion; "the first of these portions is mine, as one of the party; the second also is mine, because of my rank among beasts; the third you will yield me as a tribute to my courage and nobleness of character; while, as to the fourth — why, if any one wishes to dispute with me for it, let him begin, and we shall soon see whose it will be."

THE FOX
THAT WAS DOCKED

THERE was a cunning but over-reaching old Fox, who, having fortified himself within certain Banks for the plucking and eating of unsuspecting Geese, was, nevertheless, unearthed, and pursued by the County Hounds. Being caught by a trap in his flight, he was glad to compound for his neck by leaving his magnificent tail behind him. It was so uncouth a sight for a Fox to appear without this distinguishing ornament of his race, that the very thought of it made him weary of his life. But, however, for the better countenance of the scandal, he called the Foxes together, when he made a learned discourse upon the trouble, the uselessness, and the indecency of Foxes wearing long, draggling, bushy tails. He had no sooner finished his harangue, than up rises a cunning old Fox, who desired to be informed whether the worthy Fox that had moved against the wearing of tails gave his advice for the advantage of those that possessed such natural appendages, or to palliate the deformity and disgrace of those that had none.

THE FOX THAT WAS DOCKED.

THE DOG AND
THE SHADOW

THERE was a vain and greedy young Dog, who, coming near a certain shallow stream called Fashionable Society, saw therein the mere shadow and reflection of a tempting prize (the more so, that he conceived it the property of a luckier Dog than himself), in snapping at which he opened his mouth so eagerly and so foolishly as to cause to fall away from him a rare possession of the same kind which was his own, and which was all he could have desired for his heart's content, but which his lips were never allowed to touch more.

THE DOG AND THE SHADOW.

THE FOX AND
THE GRAPES

A LONELY She-Fox was fascinated by some grapes which hung high in a certain Vineyard, and, in order to obtain which, she for some time fatigued herself in leaps, friskings, and contortions, more or less graceful, until her joints grew stiff, and her bones fairly ached again. But at last, finding her agility decrease, and the grapes farther from her reach than ever, "Let who will take them," said she; "as for me, I would none of them at a gift, for I am sure they are as sour as vinegar."

THE FOX AND THE GRAPES.

THE FOX AND
THE STORK

THE Fox poured out some rich soup upon a flat dish, tantalising the Stork, and making him look ridiculous, for the soup, being a liquid, foiled all the efforts of his slender beak. In return for this, when the Stork invited the Fox, he brought the dinner on the table in a jug with a long narrow neck, so that while he himself easily inserted his beak and took his fill, the Fox was unable to do the same, and so was properly paid off.

"With Mr. Fox's respects &
many happy returns of the day"

"With Mr. Stork's kind regards
and the compliments of his lady."

x

[37]

THE MOLE AND
HER SON

A YOUNG conceited Mole one day prevailed upon his mother to take him out of their dwelling-hole to see some of the fine sights so much admired by the people above them. He proceeded to criticise the surrounding beauties.

"What an execrable view this is!" said he, pausing in sight of a beautiful landscape, and twirling his scanty whiskers with an air. "You don't mean to tell me that sky is blue! and the idea of purple grass is positively ridiculous. There's a horse, too, with six legs, and a man taller than his own house. And I'm sure we ought to be able to see the flowers growing in those mountains at this distance! Out of all reason, colour, and proportion. Preposterous!"

"My son, my son," said the mother, "as you are incapable of appreciating what you affect to despise, it is unfortunate that you are not dumb as well as blind, and so might have escaped this exposure of your ignorance."

THE MOLE AND HER SON.

THE CAT'S PAW

A CUNNING old Ape who felt his mouth water at the vicinity of certain tempting fruits which he longed to possess, but which he knew to be guarded in a place too warm for his fingers to venture in, asked a foolish young Cat, whom he saw passing, to come to this assistance.

"I pray you," he said, "lend me your paw to reach those pretty nice things that I require. I am a poor old creature that cannot help himself, and will well reward you for your pains."

The silly Cat compiled; but in so doing, burnt his claws so terribly that he was unable to catch mice for months to come, while the old Ape got safely off with the plunder.

THE CAT'S PAW.

THE TREACHEROUS CUR

A CERTAIN Merchant had a Dog called "Clerk," in whom he placed a particular confidence. He fed the creature from his own table, and, in short, took more care of him than of any of his fellows. This kindness, however, was but ill repaid; for, one day, no sooner was the Merchant's back turned, than the rascally hound flew to the safe, tore it open, and helped himself to all the choice bits that his benefactor, with much care, had scraped together for the sustenance of his own children. But, unfortunately, his Master returned in time to detect him in the act, and bade him prepare for punishment.

"Master," said the Cur, in excuse, "bethink you, I am one of your family. I am a Dog who has hitherto borne a good name. Punish me not for this first offence; rather turn your displeasure upon those rascals the Wolves, who make a daily practice of plunder."

"No! no!" replies his Master. "I would rather spare forty Wolves, who rob through want or evil training, than a Dog like you, who is faithless to trust and insensible to kindness."

So the Dog was bound and carried out of the house, and consigned to the mercy of deep water, with a heavy chain attached to him to keep him from finding his way back again.

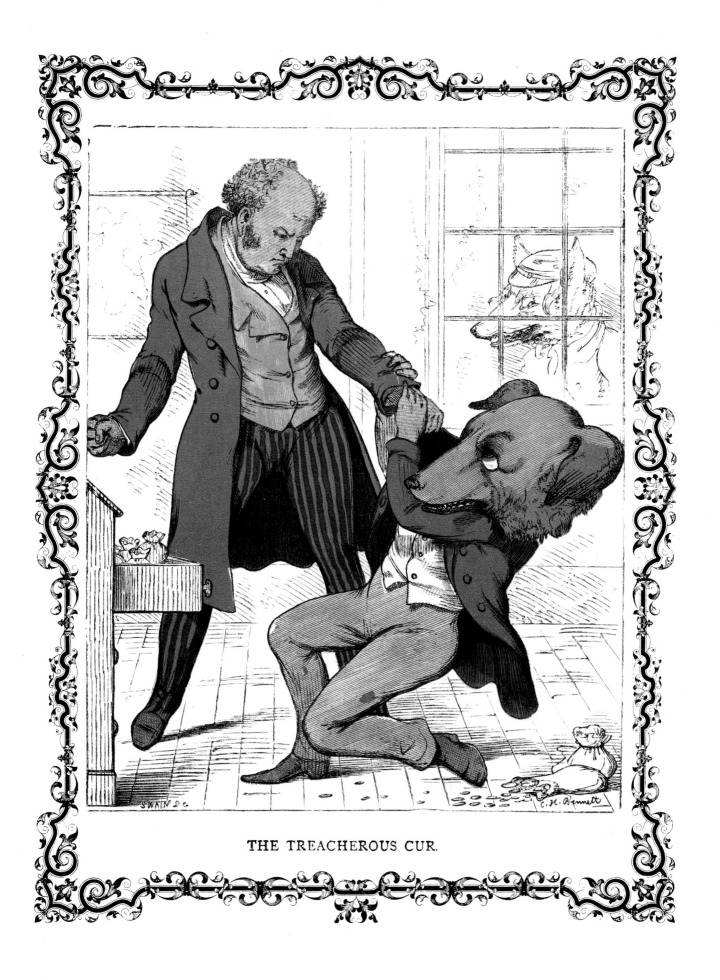

THE TREACHEROUS CUR.

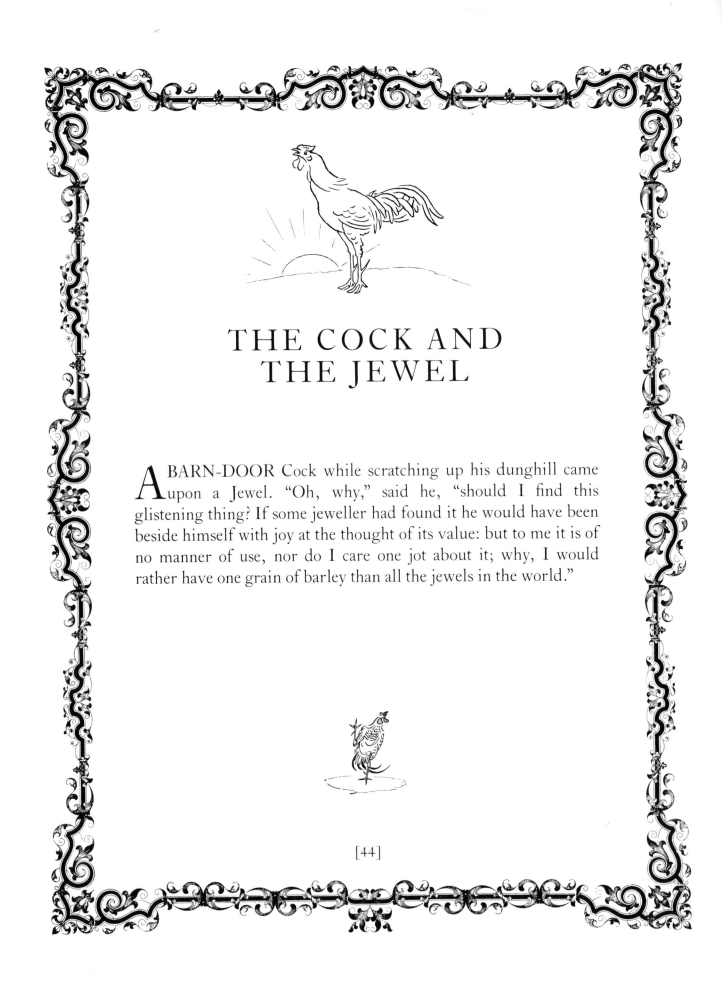

THE COCK AND
THE JEWEL

A BARN-DOOR Cock while scratching up his dunghill came upon a Jewel. "Oh, why," said he, "should I find this glistening thing? If some jeweller had found it he would have been beside himself with joy at the thought of its value: but to me it is of no manner of use, nor do I care one jot about it; why, I would rather have one grain of barley than all the jewels in the world."

THE DOG AND
THE WOLF

THERE was a gaunt, ragged gipsy of a Wolf who fell into company with a sleek, jolly Dog belonging to the Spaniel tribe, on the King's highway. The Wolf was wonderfully pleased with his companion, and was inquisitive to learn how he had brought himself to that commendable state of body.

"Why," said the Dog. "I keep my Master's house, and I have the best of meat, drink, and lodging for my pains; indeed, if you'll go along with me, and do as I do, you may fare as I fare."

The Wolf readily agreed, and so away they trotted together; but as they approached the house the Wolf caught side of the Dog's curiously embroidered collar, from which a kind of gold chain hung down over the shoulder. "Brother," said he, "what is this I see?"

"Oh, that's nothing!" says the Spaniel; "a mere social badge to let the world know whose Dog I am."

"Indeed!" says the other. "If those be the conditions, good-bye. Bare bones and independence, rather than cold chicken with a chain and dog-collar."

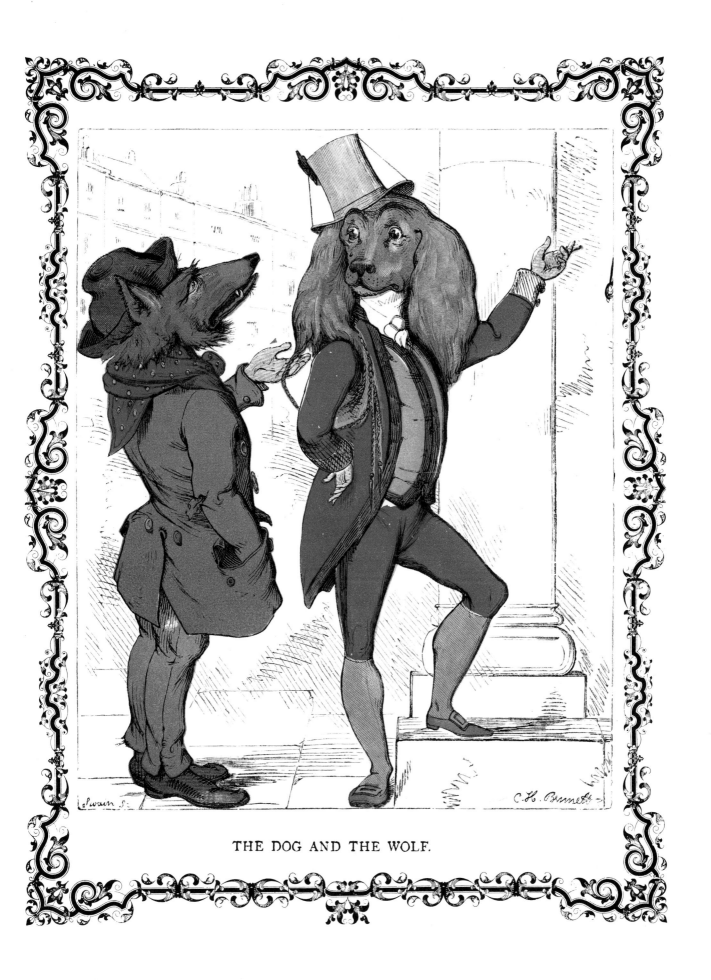

THE DOG AND THE WOLF.

THE DOG
IN THE MANGER

A CHURLISH, pampered Cur, who had a comfortable place in a gentleman's well-filled Manger, would from thence snap and snarl to frighten off all poor beasts of draught and burden who passed that way – driven by the hardness of the time of year to beg for provender they could not earn by labour in the fields. This Dog wanted for nothing himself, and yet took an ill-natured pleasure in keeping poor famishing creatures from many a meal, which, but for his officious yelping, they might have enjoyed from his Master's bounty.

THE DOG IN THE MANGER

THE HARE AND
THE TORTOISE

"WHAT a dull, heavy creature," said a bright-eyed, nimble-footed Hare, "is this same plodding Tortoise! He trudges along in the mud, neither looking to the right nor to the left, only caring to nibble such of the dryest grass and the dirtiest roots as come in his way, and making no more progress in a day's march than I can accomplish in two or three careless bounds!"

"And yet," said the Tortoise (in whose hearing the speech had been made for his humiliation), "although I have neither your lightness of foot, nor the compact and powerful symmetry of your haunches, I will undertake to run you a wager."

"Agreed!" said the Hare, contemptuously. So a goal was named, and away they started together. The Tortoise kept jogging along at his usual rate, and was soon left behind and out of sight by the Hare, who, tired of running alone in a given direction, fell to browsing on choice plants, and then went off to a game of play with certain of his sportive companions, finally making up his form for a snug nap among some tempting long autumn grass! "For," said he, "with my great natural gift of swiftness, I can fetch up Old Humdrum Master Tortoise whenever I please."

But he overslept himself, it seems. For when he came to wake, it was already dark, the weather had changed, and the fields were heavy with clay; and though he scudded away as fast as the ground would let him, he was fain to drop at last, half dead with cold and fatigue, in sight of the winning post, which the Tortoise had reached comfortably before him — thereby winning the wager.

[50]

THE HARE AND THE TORTOISE.

THE EAGLE AND
THE FOX

AN Eagle and a Fox entered into a covenant of mutual affection and resolved to live near one another, looking upon close intercourse as a way of strengthening friendship. Accordingly the former flew to the top of a high tree and built her nest, while the latter went into a bush at the foot and placed her litter there. One day, however, when the Fox was away foraging, the Eagle, being hard pressed for food, swooped down into the bush, snatched up the cubs and helped her own fledglings to devour them. When the Fox came back and saw what had happened she was not so much vexed at the death of her young ones as at the impossibility of requital. For the Eagle having wings and she none, pursuit was impossible. So she stood some distance away and did all that is left for the weak and impotent to do – poured curses on her foe. But the Eagle was not to put off for long the punishment due to her violation of the sacred tie of friendship. It happened that some country-people were sacrificing a goat, and the Eagle flew down and carried away from the altar some of the burning flesh. But when she had got it to her eyrie a strong wind got up and kindled into flame the thin dry twigs of the nest, so that the eaglets, being too young to be able to fly, were roasted, and fell to the ground. Then the Fox ran up and, before the Eagle's eyes, devoured them every one.

THE FOX AND
THE CROCODILE

THERE happened to be an argument once between a quiet cynic of a Fox and a conceited, vulgar Crocodile upon the point of Blood and Extraction; the Crocodile boasted of his descent and the renown of his ancestors.

"Our family," said he, "is of the greatest antiquity. We were princes in Egypt before the foundation of the Pyramids."

"Friend," said the Fox, smiling, and pointing with his claw to certain dabs of mud resting between the coarse excrescences of the speaker's hide, "there will need no herald to prove your gentility, for you carry the marks of your origin on your very skin."

THE FOX AND THE CROCODILE.

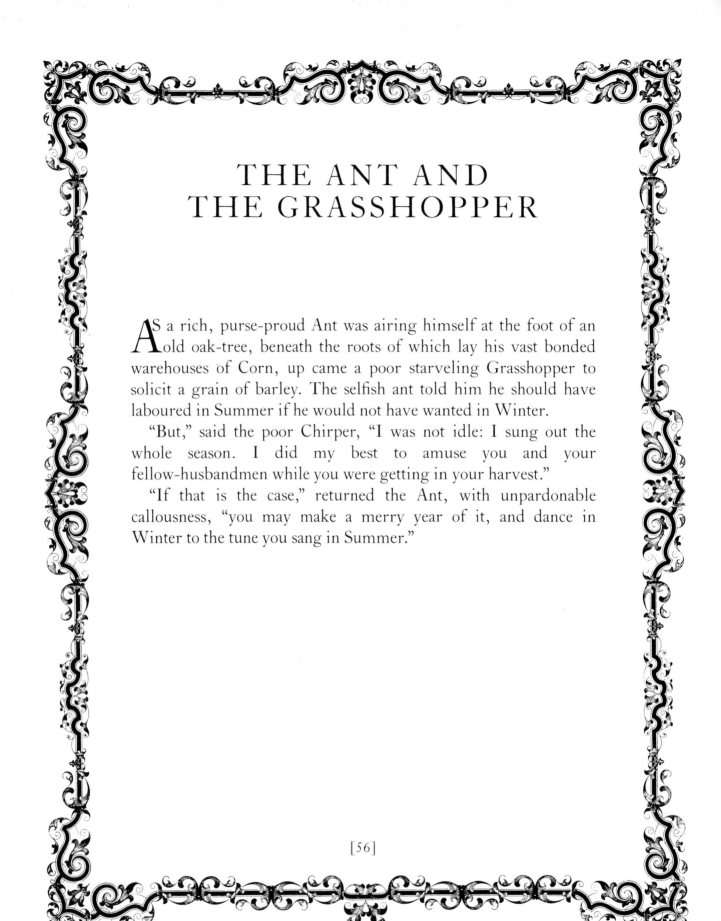

THE ANT AND
THE GRASSHOPPER

AS a rich, purse-proud Ant was airing himself at the foot of an old oak-tree, beneath the roots of which lay his vast bonded warehouses of Corn, up came a poor starveling Grasshopper to solicit a grain of barley. The selfish ant told him he should have laboured in Summer if he would not have wanted in Winter.

"But," said the poor Chirper, "I was not idle: I sung out the whole season. I did my best to amuse you and your fellow-husbandmen while you were getting in your harvest."

"If that is the case," returned the Ant, with unpardonable callousness, "you may make a merry year of it, and dance in Winter to the tune you sang in Summer."

THE ANT AND THE GRASSHOPPER.

THE WOLF
IN SHEEP'S CLOTHING

THERE is a story of a greedy Wolf, who, having deceptively wrapped himself in woollen clothing marked X25, in sign of his belonging to the peaceful flock, was, for a long while, permitted to prowl about certain homesteads, where, his real nature not being suspected, he caused most unaccountable decreases in the family store of mutton.

But being in the end discovered by the Shepherd (who was named Inspector), he was, by that watchful guardian of the public pastures, ignominiously stripped and flogged, howling to the wilderness.

"Why whip you the animal?" asked the neighbours. "Was he not faithful?"

"Faithful!" cried the Shepherd, laying on in wrath. "I took him for an honest watch-dog, and, lo! I find him in Sheep's clothing, making sheep's eyes at a foolish ewe, whom he would have eaten out of house and home to satisfy his wolfish cravings, had she not given him her Master's lamb for supper."

THE WOLF IN SHEEP'S CLOTHING.

THE HORSE AND
THE STAG

THERE was a Horse who had a meadow all to himself until a Stag came and began to injure the pasture. The Horse, eager to punish the Stag, asked a man whether there was any way of combining to do this. "Certainly," said the Man, "if you don't object to a bridle and to my mounting you with javelins in my hand." The Horse agreed, and was mounted by the Man; but, instead of being revenged on the Stag, he himself became a servant of the Man.

THE WOLF AND
THE CRANE

A RAGGED-HAIRED, sharp-fanged Wolf, having, through overgorging himself with honest men's property, brought on an uneasy sensation about his throat, which threatened to be fatal, applied to a clever Crane of the long-billed species to help him through his trouble, upon condition of a very considerable reward for the practitioner's pains. The Crane, by skilfully removing certain perilous obstructive matters, brought the Wolf's throat out of danger, and then claimed the fulfilment of his client's promise.

"What!" said the knavish brute; "have I not let you go without even the mark of my gripe round your own throttle? Be thankful that I have not mangled your lean carcase for you, stripped your head of its knowing wig, and your back of its glossy, rustling robe." Expect no greater recompense for saving the life of a Wolf.

THE WOLF AND THE CRANE.